D d D
D
D
E e
E F f
J j K K k L l l
J j p
o
o O o P p
O P
o O U u U u V v
T T
t T U U V v
U Y Z z V
t Y Z z z Z
y Y Z Z
y Y Z

This book belongs to …

_____

©Illus. Dr. Seuss 1957

Dr. Seuss's

A B C

Beginner Books

BIG A

little a

What begins with A?

3

Aunt Annie's alligator .

. . . . . A . . a . . A

BIG B

little   b

What begins with B?

Barber
baby
bubbles
and a
bumblebee.

BIG C

little   c

What begins with C?

Camel on the ceiling
C . . . . c C

10

BIG D

little   d

David Donald Doo
dreamed
a dozen doughnuts
and
a duck-dog, too.

ABCDE..e..e

ear

egg

elephant

e

e

E

15

BIG F

little   f

F . . f . . F

Four fluffy feathers
on a
Fiffer-feffer-feff.

17

ABCD
EFG

Goat
girl
googoo goggles
G . . . g . . . G

BIG H
little   h

Hungry horse.
Hay.

Hen in a hat.
Hooray !
Hooray !

BIG I

little i

i.... i.... i

Icabod
is
itchy.

So am I.

BIG J

little   j

What begins with j?

Jerry Jordan's
jelly jar
and jam
begin that way.

BIG K

little k

Kitten. Kangaroo.

Kick a kettle.
Kite
and a
king's kerchoo.

BIG L
little   l

Little Lola Lopp.
Left leg.
Lazy lion
licks a lollipop.

29

BIG M

little   m

Many mumbling mice
are making
midnight music
in the moonlight . . .

mighty nice

BIG N

little   n

What begins with those?

Nine new neckties
and a nightshirt
and a nose.

33

O is very useful.
You use it when you say:
"Oscar's only ostrich
oiled
an orange owl today."

35

...P

Painting pink pajamas.
Policeman in a pail.

Peter Pepper's puppy.
And now
Papa's in the pail.

BIG Q

little   q

What begins with Q ?

The quick
Queen of Quincy
and her
quacking quacker-oo.

QUACK
QUACK

41

BIG R

little   r

Rosy Robin Ross.

Rosy's going riding
on her
red rhinoceros.

BIG S

little　　　　s

Silly Sammy Slick
sipped six sodas
and got
sick sick sick.

45

T . . . . T
t . . . . . . t

What begins with T?

Ten tired turtles
on a tuttle-tuttle tree.

47

BIG U

little   u

What begins with U?

Uncle Ubb's umbrella
and his
underwear, too.

49

BIG V

little   v

Vera Violet Vinn
 is
very
very
very awful
on her violin.

W . . w . . W

Willy Waterloo
washes Warren Wiggins
who is
washing Waldo Woo.

X is very useful
if your name is
Nixie Knox.
It also
comes in handy
spelling ax
and extra fox.

NIXIE KNOX

BIG Y

little   y

A yawning yellow yak.
Young Yolanda Yorgenson
is yelling on his back.

QRS
TUV...

W..X
Y.. and ....

BIG Z
little z

What begins with Z?

I do.

I am a
Zizzer-Zazzer-Zuzz
as you can
plainly see.